MAGIC BEACH

Alison Lester

For Joanie

ALLEN&UNWIN

At our beach,
at our magic beach,
we swim in the sparkling sea,
surfing and splashing
   and jumping the waves,
shrieking and laughing with glee.

Wild white horses are thundering past,
racing to get to the land,
plunging and prancing and tossing their heads,
then fading away on the sand.

At our beach,
at our magic beach,
we play in the sand for hours,
digging and building,
 with buckets and spades,
invincible castles and towers.

The king and the queen are trapped in the moat,
a dragon is spitting out flames.
Princess Belinda is charging the beast
to rescue little Prince James.

At our beach,
at our magic beach,
we search in the clear, warm pools,
peering at starfish,
 limpets and crabs,
and tiny fish darting in schools.

Into the Kingdom of Fishes we go,
riding on sea-dragons' tails.
Angelfish ferry a cargo of pearls
past creeping convoys of snails.

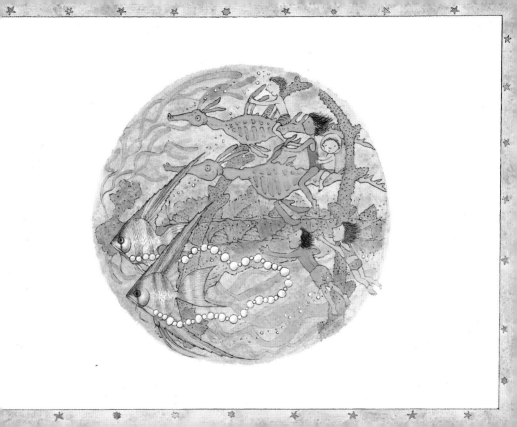

At our beach,
at our magic beach,
we walk when it's cloudy and grey,
looking for driftwood,
  feathers and shells
washed up on the edge of the bay.

A leather-bound chest with buckles of brass
lies tossed on the sand by the tide.
As we push back the lid we are dazzled by light
from the glittering treasure inside.

⌄◟◞

At our beach,
at our magic beach,
we rock in the tangerine boat,
paddling out to the end of the line,
then drifting back to the float.

The wind fills our sails as we follow the sun,
and the look-out's eyes are keen.
We'll navigate over the edge of the world
to islands where no-one has been.

At our beach,
at our magic beach,
we laze on the jetty and wait,
watching the watery shadows below
for something to nibble the bait.

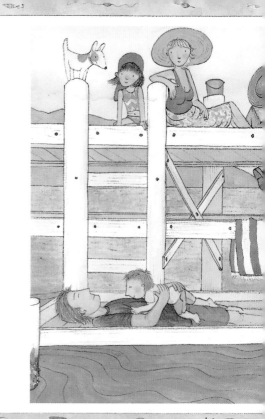

A monstrous shark has taken the hook,
it's struggling hard to break free,
thrashing and crashing and fighting the line
as we drag it in from the sea.

At our beach,
at our magic beach,
we bask in the glow of the fire.
The moon makes a silvery path
  on the sea,
and the waves come to shore
  with a sigh.

A beacon is signalling up on the cliff,
an answer blinks back from the bay.
Smugglers are hauling in crate-loads of rum,
then silently stealing away.

At our beach,
at our magic beach,
the old bed is cosy and wide.
To the sounds of the ocean
we sleep through the night . . .

. . . adrift on the evening tide.

This edition published 2007

First published 1990

Allen & Unwin
83 Alexander St
Crows Nest NSW 2065
Australia
Phone: (61 2) 8425 0100
Fax: (61 2) 9906 2218
Email: info@allenandunwin.com
Web: www.allenandunwin.com

National Library of Australia
Cataloguing-in-Publication entry:

Lester, Alison
Magic Beach.
ISBN 978 174175 268 7
1. Title.

A823.3

Set in Baskerville by Bookset

10 9 8 7 6 5 4 3 CC 14 13 12 11 10

Printed in China through Colorcraft Ltd, Hong Kong